TRANSFORMERS
ROBOTS IN DISGUISE

TRANSFORMERS
ROBOTS IN DISGUISE

Autobot
World Tour

Steve Foxe

LITTLE, BROWN AND COMPANY
New York   Boston

Little, Brown and Company

Hachette Book Group
1290 Avenue of the Americas, New York, NY 10104
Visit us at lb-kids.com

Little, Brown and Company is a division of Hachette Book Group, Inc.
The Little, Brown name and logo are trademarks of
Hachette Book Group, Inc.

The publisher is not responsible for websites (or their content)
that are not owned by the publisher.

First Edition: May 2016

ISBN 978-0-316-26684-0

10 9 8 7 6 5 4 3 2 1

RRD-C

Printed in the United States of America

Licensed By:

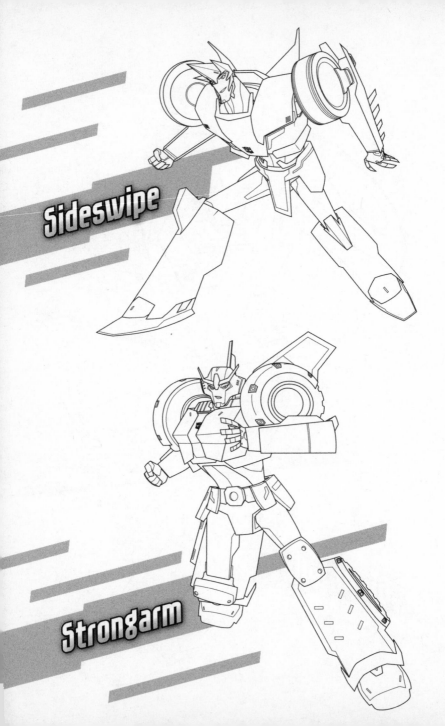

Sideswipe

Strongarm

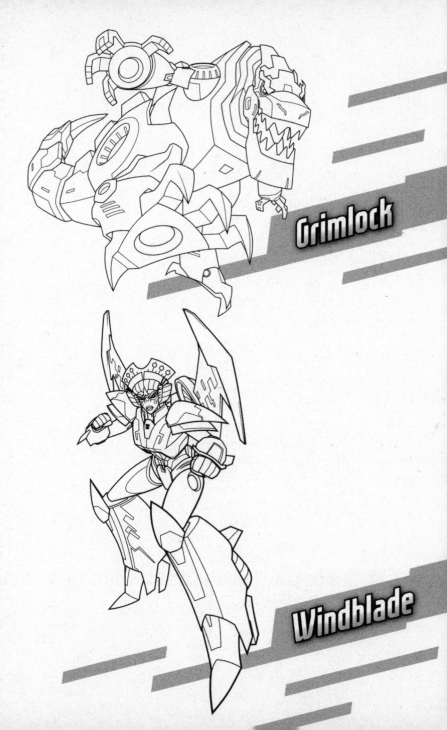

Grimlock

Windblade

Chapter 1

"**You're going down, you overgrown spark** plug!" Sideswipe shouts, leaping from branch to branch. The headstrong young Autobot is in hot pursuit of his quarry: a bug-like escaped Decepticon crackling with electricity. "After I'm done with you, you won't be able to charge up a blinking taillight!"

1

The two bots race through the rain forest undergrowth, thousands of miles away from the scrapyard that serves as the Autobots' base on Earth. Sideswipe's ninja-like acrobatics allow him to keep pace with the swiftly flying Decepticon.

When Bumblebee and Optimus Prime decided to assemble an away team to travel the world hunting down rogue Decepticons, Sideswipe was the first to volunteer. Who wants to sit around a scrapyard when there are rear axles to kick? As far as Sideswipe is concerned, he's more than a match for anybot—and eager to prove it.

The rest of his team trails behind him: legendary Autobot leader Optimus Prime; stoic samurai Drift; Drift's Mini-Con students, Slipstream and Jetstorm; and Windblade, the newest addition to the squad, sent to Earth over a thousand years ago on a secret mission to track down Decepticons.

"Hey, Slick, wait up!" Windblade shouts after Sideswipe. "We don't know what this Decepticon can do. The tree cover is so thick that we can't radio Fixit for intel." Windblade and Drift slice through vines with their swords, clearing a path for Optimus and the Mini-Cons. "No sense going into a fight blind."

"Are you kidding me?" Sideswipe yells back, barely glancing over his shoulder at his teammates. "Look at this puny bot. He can't be any more dangerous than a bug zapper."

The electrified Decepticon lets out a shrill

buzzing noise in response to Sideswipe's insult. He stops in his tracks and spreads his shiny metallic wings, revealing a vibrantly glowing battery.

Sideswipe grinds to a halt, narrowly avoiding a collision with the enemy bot.

"No one calls Shocksprocket 'puny' and gets away with it," the agitated Decepticon growls. "I'll show you what I can do, all right!"

Shocksprocket's battery pulses with a radioactive green light. Sideswipe, just moments ago lost in the thrill of the chase, takes a cautious step backward. Windblade and the other bots keep their distance.

ZZZZZZAP!

The Decepticon lets loose a massive arc of

electricity, jolting Sideswipe and turning the damp soil under the Autobots' feet into a painful carpet of shocks! As the bots twist in pain, Shocksprocket makes a break for it.

"Into the trees!" Drift shouts, pulling himself off the ground and onto a sturdy branch. His two Mini-Cons scurry up nearby trees to join their master.

"The kid's injured. We have to help him!" Windblade says. She leaps off the electrified ground and grabs hold of the vines around her.

"I'll get him," Optimus says, grimacing through the discomfort of being shocked. "I'm too heavy to climb into the trees. You just—argh!—make sure that Decepticon doesn't—ouch!—escape!"

Steeling himself, Optimus stomps toward Sideswipe while Drift, Windblade, and the Mini-Cons dash through the trees in the direction of the rapidly fleeing Shocksprocket. Optimus hoists the young bot into his arms as the final arcs of electricity die down around them.

"Sideswipe, are you all right?"

"Whoa," the young bot says, sparks dancing in front of his optics. "I need to throttle back on the Energon next time. I think I overcharged."

Optimus shakes his head in disapproval.

"Now we know what this Shocksprocket is capable of. Let's help the others take him down," Optimus says. "And this time, try not to provoke him." Sideswipe and

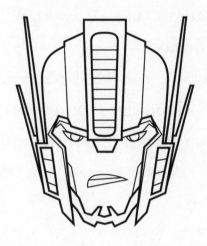

Optimus shake off any remaining effects of their unexpected jolt and sprint after their teammates. The dense jungle foliage renders their vehicle modes useless, giving the diminutive Shocksprocket an advantage as he flits between the tightly packed trees.

Before long, the Autobots are reunited in a clearing bordered on three sides by trees and on one side by a jagged wall of rock.

"Nowhere to run, Decepticon!" Optimus roars. "Surrender!"

"I'm not the one who's trapped, Autobot bully!" Shocksprocket's battery starts to hum, building up another massive charge!

"Quick, everyone back into the trees!" Drift orders.

"I'll grab Slipstream and Jetstorm," Windblade says, taking advantage of the open clearing to shift into her vehicle mode, a vertical takeoff and landing jet. Her turbines spin to life, lifting her above the tree line with the Mini-Cons clinging on below.

"Don't worry, getting bug-zapped gave me a plan!" Sideswipe says, yanking a thick branch off of a giant tree. "These Earth plants don't seem to conduct electricity, which means they should be safe to use as..."

Sideswipe leaps into the air toward Shocksprocket, bringing the heavy branch down onto the Decepticon's head.

THWAK!

"...a flyswatter!"

The hum of Shocksprocket's battery dies down, and with it the radioactive green glow. Sideswipe drops the branch next to the defeated Decepticon.

Drift and Optimus climb out of the trees. Windblade and the Mini-Cons touch back down on solid ground.

"I guess letting you get attacked is a good way to figure out a plan, Slick," Windblade says, changing back into her bot mode. She scuffs Sideswipe on the shoulder affectionately. If bots could blush, Sideswipe would be fire-engine red.

"It looks like we have signal in this clearing," Optimus says, tapping at his communicator. "I'll tell Fixit to cross another Decepticon off the wanted list while you bots get Shocksprocket into stasis."

Fixit's eager face fizzes into view on Optimus's screen.

"Hello, friend-bots! Bumblebee, Strongarm,

and Grimlock are off chasing down another Decepticon signal. My, you all stay busy!" Fixit says. "I hope you are enjoying the jumble...rumble...jungle!"

Ever since Fixit crashed to Earth in the *Alchemor* prison ship, his speech module has been a bit...off.

Sideswipe pushes his way into the frame, crowding Optimus's space.

"Actually, the heat and humidity are real

pains for my paint job. I'm worried my good looks are going to rust!"

"Well, I've got good news for you, then!" Fixit says with a smile. "Your next destination won't be humid or hot—it'll be freezing! It's approximately twenty-thousand twenty-nine feet above sea level. Set your Groundbridge to Mount Everest!"

Chapter 2

"**Mount Everest?**" Windblade says. "**Fixit,** you little bundle of loose screws, you better be kidding."

"What's so bad about some mountain?" Sideswipe asks. Windblade looks at the other bots for support, slowly realizing that they're just as unfamiliar with the fabled peak as Sideswipe.

"I sometimes forget that not every bot has been on this planet as long as I have. Mount Everest is one of the most extreme locations on Earth. Humans try to climb it to prove their bravery. Some fail—*permanently*."

"Sounds dangerous," Sideswipe says, slinking closer to Windblade. "I *like* danger."

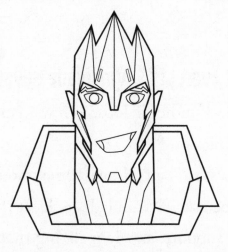

"Cool your wheels, Slick," Windblade says, glaring at the young bot.

The typically silent Drift steps forward. "As much as I regret agreeing with Sideswipe, he is correct in principle. We are much more durable than the inhabitants of this planet. I am confident that I can rise to the task." The dutiful Mini-Cons behind him nod in agreement.

"I think you mean *we* can rise to the task, buddy," Sideswipe says.

Drift does not respond.

"Enough debate, Autobots," Optimus says, putting an end to the discussion. "It is our sworn duty to protect this planet and the humans who call it home. That means going anywhere we're needed." Optimus punches at the keys on his communicator, pulling up a larger hologram of Fixit for all the bots to see. "Fixit, what kind of threat have you identified?"

"Actually, sir, I can explain that!" Russell Clay, the young son of scrapyard owner Denny Clay, pushes his way in front of Fixit. Rusty and his father are keeping the Autobots' presence a secret from the world, helping them to stay robots in disguise.

"I was watching my favorite show, *Beyond the Mysterious Unknown with Loren Fortean*, when I noticed—"

"Wait a minute," Sideswipe interrupts. "I thought your favorite show was *My Miniature Mustang?*"

"Jeez, Sideswipe, that was last week," Rusty

replies. "Try to keep up. Anyway, as I was saying, I was watching the best show on television, *Beyond the Mysterious Unknown with Loren Fortean*, where this supercool explorer, Loren Fortean, takes viewers 'beyond the veil of the known world-world-world!'"

"Optimus, your communicator is malfunctioning," Sideswipe says.

"Sideswipe! Stop interrupting me!" Rusty responds, losing his patience. "The speaker isn't broken. That's just how the opening credits go: 'world-world-world,' like an echo. Loren Fortean investigates all sorts of strange occurrences, like crop circles, the Loch Ness monster, and why those yellow snack cakes with artificial cream filling never go bad. And on his latest episode, he filmed a Decepticon!"

Optimus and the other bots exchange concerned glances. "This is very serious, Rusty. If this Fortean human exposes our battle with the Decepticons, it could put humanity in grave danger."

"That's the best part, though, Optimus— Loren Fortean has no idea that it's a bot!

Grimlock and I can recognize a Cybertronian a mile away—or on a TV screen, anyway—but the show's producers think they captured the first-ever, six-second-long footage of the yeti!"

Rusty's enthusiasm is met with more blank stares.

"I'm not familiar with that Earth animal species," Optimus says.

"That's because it doesn't exist," Rusty replies. "Or maybe it does, but we don't have proof yet. It's like a big white ape that lives in the Himalayan mountains. Only this one isn't an ape at all; he was definitely a Decepticon."

Windblade considers what Rusty has explained. "I know you trust the humans, Optimus," she says, "and I respect their contributions to our mission, but you're asking us to risk our sparks based on a human *child* thinking he saw something in a split-nanocycle frame of a remote audio/video signal. For all we know, this Fortean human doctored the footage for attention."

"No!" Rusty says, getting defensive. "Loren Fortean live-streams all his episodes, so viewers know we're getting a real look at the world beyond-beyond-beyond...."

Sideswipe chuckles. "Hey, Fixit, Rusty's starting to sound like you!"

Fixit frowns.

"Actually, sir, I was able to verify Russell Clay's suspicions," the Mini-Con pipes in. "To an extent, anyway. Our systems can't scan for accurate signals from this distance, but based on Russell's description and a scan of the footage, it looks like it may be a Decepticon called Abominus."

Windblade slaps her palm to her forehead. "Scrap!"

"You know this guy, Windy?" Sideswipe asks, cocking his thumb at the hologram Fixit has provided. Abominus is a bulky, long-limbed, ape-like Decepticon, with a blindingly white paint job. His face is framed with armor plating that gives him more than a passing resemblance to an albino orangutan.

"First, don't call me 'Windy,'" Windblade replies. "Second, yes, unfortunately I do. Eons ago, before I came to Earth, I helped arrest him. Abominus is a hermit and a technical genius. He's obsessed with living off the grid and is willing to build any weapons he needs to defend his stronghold. He'll blast anyone who even looks at his bunker the wrong way, and he has a real problem with authority."

Sideswipe sidles up next to Drift and whispers into his audio receptor. "Good thing we're not bringing Strongarm with us then, right?" Once again, Drift ignores the young Autobot's comments.

Rusty's face reappears on the hologram. "You have to protect Loren Fortean and his crew before this bad bot blows them all up!"

Optimus and the other bots exchange solemn nods, with the exception of Sideswipe, who is unable to hide his excitement at the prospect of another daring adventure. The

Autobot leader reassures Rusty that everything is going to be okay. "Do not worry,
Rusty. We'll apprehend Abominus before he
can harm Fortean and his crew—or expose
our existence to the world!"

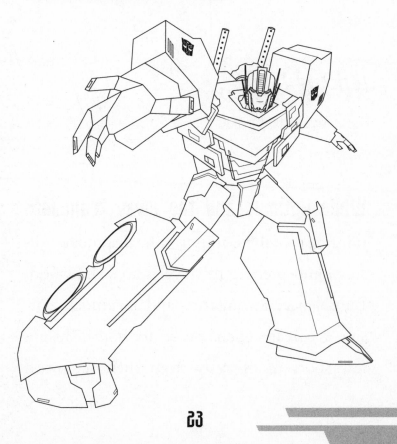

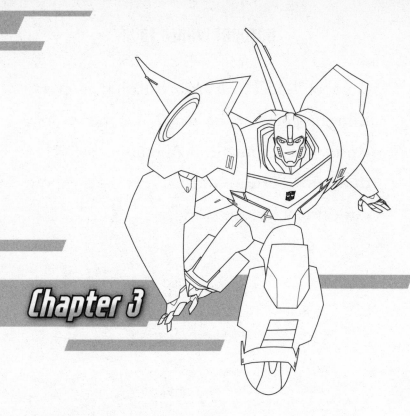

Chapter 3

While Optimus and the away team lock rainforest rabble-rouser Shocksprocket in stasis and prepare to travel across the world, Bumblebee, Strongarm, and Grimlock pursue a threat much closer to home. Just a few short miles away from their scrapyard headquarters, the bots are closing in on a Decepticon signal moving at a glacial pace.

"Sir, I have a bad feeling about this," Strongarm says to Bumblebee. A cadet from Cybertron, Strongarm loves rules and order. She'll take the cautious route every time—and hold it over Sideswipe's head when his riskier decisions bite him in the tailpipe. "A signal this close to the command center should have shown up weeks ago, unless the Decepticon has been perfectly still since the crash."

Grimlock stomps up next to Bumblebee and Strongarm. The latter two bots have convenient Earth vehicle modes that allow them to get around inhabited areas without arousing suspicion. However, Grimlock's other mode is a fearsome Dinobot, meaning he can only cut loose when he's out of human sight.

"Maybe a giant piece of the ship landed right on his stabilizers. *BOOM! CRASH!*" Grimlock says, exaggerating the sound effects. "And this bot's been surviving on scrap metal and Energon leaks, waiting for one of his evil buddies to come rescue him!"

"Grimlock has a good point, Strongarm, although I think he made it on accident...." Bumblebee replies, zooming along in his yellow-and-black sports car mode. "If this signal does belong to an injured Decepticon, we have a responsibility to repair him before we lock him in stasis. These criminals deserve their sentences, but that doesn't mean we can neglect their diagnostics."

The Autobot trio clips through the woods at a fast pace. Before long, they arrive at the source of the signal: a cracked stasis pod wedged between a tumble of fallen tree trunks and debris from the ship. Strongarm changes from her police cruiser form back into bot mode, pulls out her blaster, and ducks behind a tree to cover her teammates.

"Sir," Strongarm whispers, "do you see anything?"

Bumblebee darts his optics around the crash site. The signal definitely led to this spot, but there's no Decepticon in sight.

"Negative. I'm going in," Bumblebee whispers back. "Watch my back!" The courageous Autobot leader sprints toward the downed pod, blaster in hand. Bumblebee peeks over the rim and through the shattered lid to find...a Decepticon lying in wait!

"Freeze!" Bumblebee shouts, pointing his blaster at the prone bot. The Decepticon has a large, round face and elongated arms ending in a trio of dangerously sharp claws.

Even with the commotion, his optics remain closed. He's been lying in place so long that moss has begun to grow on his exterior. "Step out of the pod with your, uhh, really pointy claws where I can see them."

The Decepticon gives no response. By now, Strongarm and Grimlock have crept up to join their leader. Grimlock lifts a massive finger and pokes the stasis chamber.

"Hello, anyone home in there?" he bellows. "Wake up, slag-heap!" The Dinobot pushes on the chamber with more force, rocking it back and forth. Still nothing from the Decepticon.

"Sir," Strongarm says in hushed tones, "maybe this prisoner was...deactivated in the crash." The trio of Autobots leans over the stasis pod, considering Strongarm's assessment. Before Bumblebee can agree, however, the Decepticon's optics slowly widen.

"Good morning, bro-bots," he says. He opens his mouth in a wide, yawn-like motion. "That power-down was exactly what I needed. I feel so . . . relaxed."

The Autobots exchange puzzled looks.

"Uhh, should I stomp him now?" Grimlock asks.

"Whoa, who needs to do any stomping?" the Decepticon replies. He stretches his long arms in a slow arc, flexing his claws. The Autobots all take a defensive step backward, but the Decepticon only digs the impressive blades into the rim of the stasis pod, pulling himself up into a sitting position. "Let's all just, like, *chill.*"

Strongarm steadies her blaster. "You're under arrest, Decepticon. You can 'chill' in an undamaged stasis pod."

"Yo, bro-bot, why do you have to harsh my vibe like that?" he responds.

This strange, new Decepticon is really trying Grimlock's patience.

"C'mon, Bee, what are we waiting for? Let

me stomp this guy already! Listening to him makes me feel like I've got brain rust!"

Before the Autobots can make a move—stomping or otherwise—the Decepticon's optics start to flash with a kaleidoscope of colors. Strongarm, Bumblebee, and Grimlock are helpless to look away.

"I tried to do this the chill way, bro-bots, but you forced my hand," the Decepticon says, optics still flashing. "Now repeat after me, 'I don't wanna arrest my buddy Brakepad.'"

"I don't wanna arrest my buddy Brakepad," the bots say in unison.

"Let's all just, like, hang out," Brakepad says.

The Autobots mimic his words, locked in

a hypnotized state. "Let's all just, like, hang out."

Brakepad's optics stop flashing, and the Autobots slump to the ground as if their power had been drained. With the heroic bots temporarily incapacitated, Brakepad slowly crawls away from the crash site, heaving his body forward using his massive claws.

By the time the Autobots snap out of their trance, the Decepticon is long gone—and so is their energy!

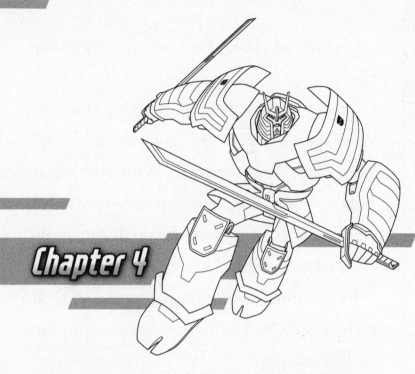

Chapter 4

Thousands of miles away, a Groundbridge portal opens up on the side of a snowy mountain. Optimus, Windblade, Sideswipe, Drift, and his Mini-Cons step through it, finding themselves at the base of a massive incline.

"Whoa, can you imagine surfing down that slope?" Sideswipe asks, miming a surfer's stance.

"I can imagine you ending up a pile of spare parts if you tried it, Slick," Windblade replies. "This is as far up the mountain as I can safely take us with the Groundbridge. The rest, we have to climb."

Optimus taps at his communicator and pulls up a fuzzy image of Fixit.

"Hello again, friends!" the Mini-Con intones through the static. "You won't get much single...shingle...SIGNAL on the mountain, but I wanted to warn you about—" The feed disappears. Optimus shakes his communicator, bringing it back to life. "...could trigger...valanches, so be caref…when you…or cause…disaster! Good luck!"

"Yeesh, that wasn't ominous at all," Sideswipe says.

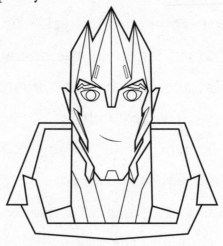

"Our vehicle forms won't be of much use here," Optimus explains, briefing the team. "The terrain is too steep and rocky for our wheeled modes, and the crosswinds are too furious for Windblade to safely maneuver.

We'll need to use our winter camo to blend in with the snow and prevent the humans' television crew from filming us. Our job is to get in, take down Abominus, and make sure the humans make it back down the mountain safely."

The bots don their winter camo, instantly replacing their vibrantly colored paint jobs with white-and-gray mottling that conceals them against the icy landscape.

"Do you want to hold down the fort here, sir?" Windblade asks Optimus. "The climb is going to get more treacherous as we go."

"I'll be fine, soldier," Optimus snaps back. Optimus was weakened in a recent battle, sacrificing part of his power to save the planet. Although he won't admit it to the other bots, he's self-conscious about his diminished strength. Windblade does her best to keep an eye on her respected commander while he returns to full power.

With the plan clear, the bots begin their trek up the mountain. Fixit's long-range signal may not reach this remote location, but the bots' close-range sensors—and Windblade's impressive intuition—tell them that a Decepticon is nearby in one direction: up. As for the humans, the bots just have to keep their optics peeled.

What starts as a hike soon turns into a climb, with the bots digging their hands into the mountainside to pull themselves up and along. "You know, Windy really made this sound more extreme," Sideswipe says, pulling himself over a ledge. "It's actually kind of... boring?"

"We're still close to the base of the mountain, Slick," Windblade replies. "You'll be begging for these bunny slopes once we reach the summit."

As the incline steepens, Drift and his Mini-Cons take the lead, using their weapons to carve easier handholds into the rock. The farther up the mountain they climb, the heavier it begins to snow, blanketing the bots in a thick white haze and obscuring their vision. Drift pulls himself over another ledge—and comes face-to-face with a laser turret!

ZAP!

Drift barely dodges the blast, slipping

to the side behind a snow bank. The turret pivots to Drift's hiding place. The Autobot shouts at his teammates to stay below the crest of the ledge.

"Drift, what's happening?" Optimus asks as another laser blast cuts through the heavy snow. "We're coming up!"

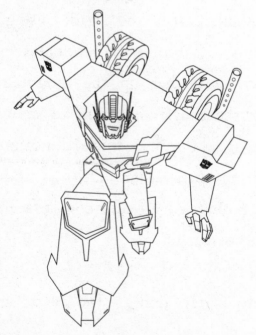

"No!" Drift yells back, nimbly dodging yet another blast. Drift leaps through the snow and slices the turret in two with his blade. Optimus, Sideswipe, Windblade, and the Mini-Cons hear the crunch of the metal being cleaved and climb up to make sure Drift is okay.

"Scrud, that looks like Abominus's handiwork, all right," Windblade says, inspecting the destroyed defensive weaponry. She has to shout to be heard over the rush of snow and wind. "This must mean we're getting closer. He probably has this entire section of the mountain booby-trapped!"

Sideswipe looks back over the ledge they just climbed. It would be a long way down if one of Abominus's traps sent the bots tumbling off the mountain. A *very* long way down.

"There's no way we can find all his traps in conditions like this," Optimus shouts. "We need to pick up the pace and disable them at the source, before that human Rusty watches on the television stumbles into one!"

Back on the outskirts of Crown City, Rusty

flips stations on the vintage television his dad installed in the diner they call home. Denny Clay is fussing around with retro soundtracks on an antique record player in the other room, filling the scrapyard with thrilling chase music, romantic interludes, and staccato horror music.

"Can you turn it down, Dad?" Rusty shouts, not budging from his place on the sofa. "Or at least pick a record? It sounds like I'm about to be attacked by a masked murderer on a date to the racetrack."

Denny pokes his head in. "That sounds like a bodacious movie. I wish it existed! But if the sound is bothering you, I just got a box of novelty oversized sunglasses I can polish." Denny pulls a huge pair of glasses from behind his back and holds them against his face. "How cool are these babies?"

"Real cool, Dad." Rusty keeps flipping channels, unenthused by his dad's new find. He's surprised when he lands on *Beyond the Mysterious Unknown with Loren Fortean*, broadcasting outside its regularly scheduled spot.

"Good afternoon, faithful viewers," Loren Fortean says, decked out in cold-weather gear and holding the mic close to his face to block the wind. "It's your host, Loren Fortean, live-streaming a very important moment from . . . *beyond the mysterious unknown!*"

Rusty leans forward, eyes glued to the screen.

"Just moments ago, my crew and I got a glimpse at what we believe to be an entire family of yeti scaling Mount Everest. Unfortunately, we swung the camera around too slowly to catch them on film, but we do have a strange phenomenon to share with you, my most loyal followers."

Fortean's cameraman pans upward, zooming in on a cliff blurred by raging snow. As the camera focuses, a massive blast of red laser light shoots through the snow, followed by another one and then a small explosion. The heavy precipitation leaves it impossible to make out anything else.

"Are the yeti performing some sort of

strange, electronic dance ceremony?" Fortean asks as the camera returns to his cold-reddened face. "Have they mastered the art of the laser light show? Don't fret over these questions, faithful audience. I, Loren Fortean, am dedicated to sharing the truth with you! My crew and I are diverting from our course to track down the source of these lights. Tune in soon for more...*Beyond the Mysterious Unknown with Loren Fortean!*"

Rusty exhales, realizing he was holding his breath throughout the entire segment.

"Uh-oh. That's not good."

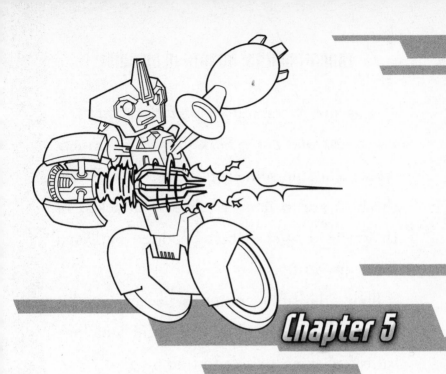

Chapter 5

"Fixit, we need to radio the bots!" Rusty
shouts, running into the command center.

"Which ones, Russell Clay?" Fixit asks.
"How nice that our team has expanded
enough that I can ask that! Like one big
Autobot family!"

"The away team, Fixit," Rusty clarifies.

"I was just watching *Beyond the Mysterious Unknown with Loren Fortean*, and his camera crew picked up some sort of laser fire. Either the bots are in danger of being attacked or they're in danger of being spotted by Loren Fortean—or both!"

Fixit dutifully punches away at his command console. The communicator logo spins and spins, unable to find a signal.

"I am sorry. The atmospheric conditions surrounding the away team are too intense. Optimus's communicator isn't picking up my message."

Rusty scrunches up his face in thought. "Wait a minute, if Cybertronian technology can't get through the bad weather, how is

Loren Fortean live-streaming from the same location as the bots?"

"Hmm, that is curious," the Mini-Con replies, returning to his screen. "Let me see if I can zero in on this human's signal instead....Aha, got it! It appears that your television human has an extensive series of relays placed around the mountain, amplifying his transmission strength. He's leaving one every hundred feet or so." Rusty shoots Fixit a hopeful look, but the Mini-Con shakes his head somberly. "I can hack into it, but not without alerting the humans. Our friends are on their own!"

"Tell me you got that, Ernie," Loren Fortean says, dropping the mic.

"Sure did, boss," Ernie, the cameraman, replies. "You can see those laser lights real well."

"Not the lights, you brute," Fortean snaps. "I just had my teeth whitened, and I was trying to show them off during that segment." Despite the brutal wind and punishing cold, Fortean still manages to flash a Hollywood-ready gigawatt smile. His pearly white teeth perfectly match the swirling snow. "My agent said it'd look good to the producers, help show them I'm ready for a better time slot than these commercial-length fillers they have me doing now."

Fortean, Ernie, and their mountaineering guide, Brigadier Wilson, pack up their hefty equipment.

"Humph, do you even care about these missing links you're chasing after?" Brigadier Wilson asks, slinging a pack over his burly shoulders. Wilson knows the mountain like the back of his well-worn hand, but he has no time to suffer Hollywood foolishness. "Seems to me you just like the attention. And I'm betting these lights you think you saw were just tricks of the sun flashing off the ice."

"Of course I care," Fortean replies. "But I've done twenty-six episodes without actually finding anything and the studio is getting restless. This expedition is my last shot. Hiring you and funding all of these live-streaming relays cost a small fortune. If I don't come back with proof of *something*, I'm washed up, finished, kaput!" Fortean trades his expensive new smile for an exaggerated frown. "That's why we have to find whatever's shooting off those lights—and make sure I look ready for prime time when we do."

Brigadier Wilson shakes his head disapprovingly, drives another signal relay into the frozen ground, and begins the trek farther up the summit.

Higher up the mountain, Drift and his Mini-Cons, Sideswipe, Optimus, and Windblade have resumed their climb. Since stumbling across the first ambush, the Autobots have sliced through two more laser turrets, blasted a hidden nest of armor-piercing nanodrones, and narrowly dodged a set of spinning saw blades equipped with nova-hot heated tips.

"So climbing this thing is a big deal to humans?" Sideswipe asks. "If you factor out Abominus's toys, it seems pretty easy to me."

Windblade scoffs. "Keep telling yourself

that, Slick. Won't seem so easy if you slip and end up tumbling into a crevice full of ice spikes where we couldn't reach you. Over time, the cold would slowly bring your gears to a halt. After a few substantial snowfalls, you'd be lost forever, just another forgotten part of the mountain."

"Wow, dramatic much?" Sideswipe responds, wincing at Windblade's grim imagination.

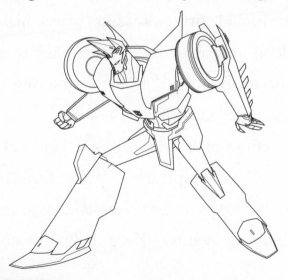

"I could do this blindfolded with a bad case of carburetor congestion." To prove his skill, the headstrong young bot swings his lower half up and lands on a rocky outcropping ahead of the other bots. "Boom!" he shouts.

As Sideswipe strikes a triumphant pose, the mountain around him starts to rumble. His optics dart around, prepared for a fight with another one of Abominus's traps. Drift, Optimus, Windblade, and the Mini-Cons join the young bot on the rock shelf, weapons drawn.

Optimus warns the other bots to prepare themselves, but there is no target in sight. The rumbling noise increases, as if a speeding train were bearing down on their location.

"Wait a nanocycle," Windblade says, audio receptors listening attentively to the growing vibration. "I don't think that's the sound of a trap—I think Sideswipe just triggered an avalanche!"

Windblade barely has time to warn the other bots before they're engulfed in a rushing torrent of heavy snow and falling rocks, knocking them all off the cliff!

"Oh, scrud!" Sideswipe yells, tumbling head over treads as he plummets down the mountainside. The quick-acting bot jams his blades into the rock to slow his descent. He blinks through the barrage to see Windblade fly past in her vehicle mode.

Windblade struggles against the heavy wind. "Grab hold!" she shouts at Optimus's tumbling form. Before sacrificing a portion of his spark to protect Earth, Optimus would have been the one heroically rescuing his teammates. Now he's the one who needs saving! But he's far too heavy for Windblade, and they both begin to fall. "You're too big! I'm sorry, Optimus!"

Windblade barely manages to steer them away from the crushing avalanche and the falling debris. Her quick thinking allows them to crash into a bank of snow on the other side of the danger.

The disaster ends as quickly as it began. As the snow clears, the Autobots look around to take stock of their teammates. Windblade and Optimus have landed on stable ground far below. Drift and Sideswipe both cling to the side of the mountain with their blades jammed firmly into the rocks. Jetstorm clings to his master's back—but Slipstream is nowhere to be found!

Chapter 6

While the away team risks their sparks, the home team of Bumblebee, Strongarm, and Grimlock can barely muster the energy to trudge back to the scrapyard. They've faced Energon vampires before, but the sloth-like Decepticon Brakepad left the bots with an entirely new sensation: laziness.

"We're back, I guess," Bumblebee mumbles, walking through the main gate. Fixit and Rusty rush over to greet the bots and update them on the laser light spotting and signal issues.

"Bee!" Rusty exclaims. "There's so much to tell you. So I was watching the show *Beyond the—*"

"Whoa," Strongarm says, cutting him off. "You are talking way too fast, Rusty. You're really bumming me out. What's the rush?"

Rusty and Fixit look at each other with concern. Strongarm is normally the rigid rule master, following protocol to a fault. Since when does she get "bummed out"?

"Bee, what's wrong with Strongarm?" Rusty asks. "Is she a clone or a hologram or a victim of mind control?" Nothing is out of the question when you live with a squad of Autobots. "Did she get possessed by a ghost-bot or something?"

Bumblebee waves off Rusty's line of questioning. "You humans are way too tense. You need to learn how to relax."

"But, sir, the away team is currently in one of the most dangerous natural locations on this planet, hunting a known criminal without any way to contact us," Fixit reminds his leader. "All while attempting to avoid television crews and exposing our existence to the human popsicle…pinnacle…POPULACE!"

"Eh, sounds like a normal day around here," Grimlock chimes in, stomping his way

past the gathering. "Boot me up if anything really interesting happens. I'm going to enjoy some rest mode until then."

"Wait, what happened to the Decepticon you were hunting down?" Rusty asks, puzzled by his friends' behavior. "Did you catch him? Where is he?"

"What does it matter?" Strongarm responds. "We catch them and they just escape again. Might as well make it easier on all of us and stop trying."

At this comment, Rusty is ready to tear out his hair. Something is clearly *very* wrong with his friends. "Can you at least tell us his name before you all power down?"

Bumblebee mumbles an answer to Rusty before he and Strongarm wander off to follow Grimlock. "Seemed like he'd be a chill bro-bot to kick it with sometime. I think his name was Brakepad."

"Oh my," Fixit whispers to Rusty. "That explains everything."

Once Strongarm, Bumblebee, and Grimlock get situated around the scrapyard, settling in for the Autobot equivalent of a lazy mid-afternoon nap, Rusty grabs his father and follows Fixit to the command center. The hardworking Mini-Con types away at the console and pulls up the profile for Brakepad.

"So he's the reason the bots are acting so funny?" Denny asks, getting up to speed on what's going on. "He looks dangerous with those giant claws of his."

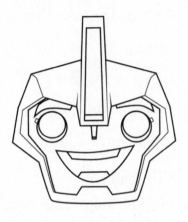

"Oh, those claws are just for show," Fixit responds. "That's why they're so shiny and sharp—he never uses them in battle. Brakepad was a very successful thief back on Cybertron. His optics emit a powerful hypnotic laser light that makes everybot in his line of sight obey his every command.

The mind-control effects wear off as soon as he leaves the vicinity, but they leave behind a powerful feeling of laziness that takes several cycles to dissipate."

"That explains why Bee and the others don't seem to care about anything," Rusty says. "They must have found Brakepad and had their energy sapped!"

"So how do we snap the bots out of it and make sure this doesn't happen the next time they try to capture Brakepad?" Denny asks.

Fixit knits his optics together in thought and resumes tapping away at his console. "Aha!" he exclaims.

"Did you find something?" Rusty asks.

"Yes!" Fixit responds. "The prisoner

manifest includes instructions on how to dampen Brakepad's powers. There's a simple machine that loops the signals he gives off and puts *him* into a deep sleep instead of affecting other bots."

"That's perfect!" Denny replies. "How do we get started?"

Fixit frowns. "We would need several component parts that aren't available in this solar system. Fortunately, it looks like Brakepad's signal hasn't moved far from his original pod. His laziness is legendary. It's unlikely he will become a pressing threat to Crown City before Bumblebee, Strongarm, and Grimlock shake off the effects of his powers. Although they won't be able to get close to him again without getting lazy all over again...."

Rusty looks at his dad for a moment. "Fixit, did you say that Brakepad never uses his sharp claws and is famous for being slow?"

"I did, Russell Clay. He is only an effective thief because other bots can't resist his power-sapping hypnotic vision."

"So a bot that couldn't see him would be immune, right?"

"That seems to make sense, yes," Fixit replies.

"Dad, you may not like this," Rusty says, "but I think I have a plan for how the two of us can capture this Decepticon. And we're going to need your new toys and a gallon of black paint to pull it off!"

Chapter 7

Back on the mountain, Drift and Sideswipe
withdraw their swords from the cliff wall and
drop down to reunite with Windblade and
Optimus. All the bots are feeling worse for
wear after that tumble.

As soon as Drift's treads touch solid ice,

Jetstorm leaps off and looks around for his fellow Mini-Con Slipstream.

"Brother!" Jetstorm yells. "Where are you, brother?"

Windblade rushes to shush the distraught Mini-Con. "We'll find your brother, little guy, but we can't risk triggering another avalanche. We need to check our volume for the rest of the climb. That means you, too, Slick."

Sideswipe turns away, hiding his guilty expression.

Jetstorm pulls out his nunchackus and hacks away at the snow and ice, digging wildly to find his brother. The other bots join in, searching the surrounding area. Minutes pass without any sign of Slipstream.

"Don't worry, Jetstorm," Sideswipe says, moving snow away in huge handfuls. "You guys are tough little bots. A little tumble like that couldn't hurt Slipstream." Jetstorm largely ignores Sideswipe's attempts at reassurance.

After a few more minutes of digging, Drift, mentor to both Mini-Cons, sheathes his sword and whispers something to Jetstorm. The other bots watch as Jetstorm's expression turns from panic to disappointment and finally to something like resignation.

"I have spoken to my student," Drift says to the group. "He understands that our mission takes priority. I have personally trained Slipstream and trust in his ability to survive until we make our way back down the mountain victorious."

Optimus moves to protest. "We don't leave bots behind, Drift. I'm field commander, and I say we don't move forward until everybot moves forward."

Before Drift can argue, Jetstorm steps up. "Master Drift is right, sir. My brother would not want to jeopardize the mission. With all respect, I ask that we hurry to our goal and then return to find Slipstream."

Optimus doesn't like what he's hearing, but looking up at the climb still to come— including the ground they lost during their fall—he knows they have to push forward. He latches onto the nearest handhold and leads what's left of his team back up the mountain.

Meanwhile, a few hundred feet away on another side of the summit, Slipstream pokes his head out of the snow and peers around. During the avalanche, a falling chunk of stone sent him spinning away from the other bots. He used his staff to slow his descent, preventing him from dropping into a crevice or careening down the entire mountain.

"Jetstorm?" Slipstream asks tentatively. "Master Drift? Sideswipe?" The Mini-Con turns around and around, spotting no one. "...Anybot?"

For a nanocycle, Slipstream feels panic setting in. Then he remembers Master Drift's teachings. Slipstream folds himself into a meditative pose. He shuts out the rushing wind and focuses on his situation.

Either you've been separated from your brother, your master, and the other bots or they've been trapped and you're on your own to complete the mission, he thinks to himself. *If you have been separated, the bots will know to carry on with the mission. You can meet them at the top of the mountain. And if they have been trapped or captured, it is your duty to defeat Abominus alone!*

Before he can press on with his mission, Slipstream hears a voice somewhere behind him. It must be the other bots! Slipstream rushes toward the direction of the voice, down a slope from where he just landed.

"I told you, if we go off-trail, I'm not

legally responsible for what happens to you!" a human voice says. Slipstream swallows his disappointment and ducks behind a snowbank. With his winter camouflage, he easily blends into the scenery.

"And I told *you*, if I don't get some decent footage, I'm getting canceled. Who knows if the studio will even bother paying the rest of your fee!"

From his hiding spot, Slipstream sees that there are three humans: a large, mustachioed man leading the way; a man with an artificial tan in the middle; and an older fellow lugging a camera bringing up the rear. All three have heavy packs strapped to their backs and look various kinds of miserable.

"If you're going to threaten my paycheck,

I'll leave you right here and now," the man with the mustache says. At this, the older cameraman looks worried.

"Uh, boss," he whispers to the man in the middle. "Maybe we should listen to Brigadier Wilson and just stick to the path. My camera has a real nice zoom; we can still get your footage."

The man in the middle looks ready to explode.

"Fine! We'll just rename the show *The Final Days of Loren Fortean* with me, your soon-to-be-unemployed host, Loren Fortean!"

Slipstream's suspicions were correct—it's the humans Rusty told them about!

"Fine!" the man they called Brigadier Wilson whisper-shouts. "You want to go off-trail so badly, I'll take you—under two conditions. One: No more yelling. We're getting into avalanche territory, and I'm not going to dig you out if you bring half the mountain down on us."

"Fine," Fortean responds. He looks huffy, like a child who isn't getting his way.

"And two: If we get footage of your mythical yeti, or anything else unusual, you pay me double."

"Double!" Fortean shouts at the top of his voice. Wilson shoots him a dangerous look. "Double?" Fortean asks again, remembering to whisper.

"Double. Or I turn around now." Brigadier Wilson crosses his arms, refusing to budge.

"Fine, double—*if* we get footage that will help me save my show."

The two humans shake over their new terms and resume their hike. Slipstream digs into the snow out of their sight. They may be on the hunt for footage, but Slipstream is determined not to be their new movie star!

Chapter 8

"Do we have to drive all the way back
through the woods?" Strongarm whines.
Rusty Clay sits in the passenger seat of
her police cruiser as they drive along at a
mere five miles per hour. "I just want to
relax."

"Yeah, me too!" Grimlock complains from his position in the trailer bed behind them.

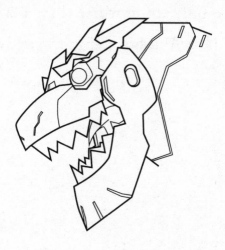

"You're not even walking, Grim," Bumblebee replies. *"I'm* the one pulling a trailer with a new stasis pod and a whining Dinobot."

"Gosh, you Autobots sure can complain," Rusty says.

"They remind me of when you were a toddler who didn't get his nap time—talk about fussy!" Denny Clay says from the passenger window of Bumblebee's vehicle. "I guess the only thing worse than a lazy Autobot is a lazy Autobot being forced to rev up and roll out."

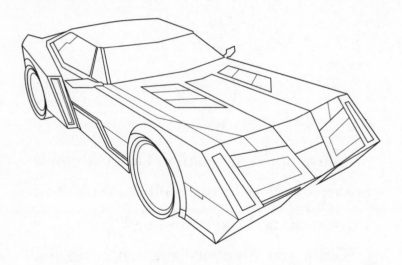

After Fixit gave Rusty and Denny a crash course in Brakepad's energy-sapping powers, Rusty devised a plan to take down the

Decepticon and free his friends from their laziness funk. Now if only he can get the bots to speed up!

"Can't you guys go a little faster?" Rusty pleads. Strongarm responds by slowing down even further. "At the rate we're going, Brakepad will make it back to Cybertron before we catch up to him."

Bumblebee revs his motor and pulls ahead. "Fine, I'll go faster, even though you're making me carry everything in the trailer. Who knew leading the Autobots would be so exhausting...?"

After a laborious trek full of complaining, Rusty and the others arrive at the crashed stasis pod that once held Brakepad. Rusty leaps out of Strongarm's passenger seat with his backpack on. "Okay, Dad, I'm going to look around—"

"No way, kiddo," Denny interrupts. He steps out of Bumblebee with a bag of his own. "Slow or not, Decepticons are too dangerous. Help Strongarm unload the stasis pod while Bee and I take a look around."

"What about me?" Grimlock asks.

"You just keep relaxing, Grim," Rusty replies. The Dinobot looks pleased with this response, while Bee and Strongarm change back into their robot forms.

Denny asks Bumblebee to hoist him up onto his shoulder so the pair can look around more easily. The Autobot and his human companion walk a slow circle around the malfunctioning prison pod before Denny spots their target.

"Bee, look over there!" Denny points to a large chunk of wreckage sticking out of the ground. Brakepad clings to the bottom with his massive claws, slowly chewing a piece of metal debris.

"So what do you want me to do about it?" Bumblebee responds. "Looks like I'm here, and he's *way* over there."

"That Decepticon has mind-control powers," Denny explains, trying to figure out a way to persuade the laziness-afflicted Bumblebee into action. "If we don't take him down, he might make you work for him. That doesn't sound very relaxing, does it?"

Bumblebee grumbles in agreement.

"Rusty, how's that stasis pod looking?" Denny shouts to his son.

Rusty is sitting on Strongarm's shoulder, directing her as she pulls the pod off the trailer inch by inch. "Almost there! Hurry it up, Strongarm. You heard my dad, if we don't capture this bot, he might make you do work like this *all* the time."

"No way, I need my rest cycle!" the typically eager-to-please cadet responds. Once the pod is fully off the trailer, Strongarm shuffles her treads to join Bumblebee near Brakepad's hanging spot.

"Hey, you!" Rusty yells up at the lounging bot. "We're taking you down!"

Brakepad stirs slightly in his perch. He turns his around head to stare at the squeaky human interrupting his rest. "Whoa, no need to shout. You're ruining my zen."

"Quick, Autobots, attack!" Denny commands from his place on Bumblebee's shoulder. The bots are slow to respond. They halfheartedly raise their arms to swing at Brakepad, but the Decepticon has more than enough time to pull himself out of harm's way.

"Bummer, bro-bots, I thought you were

cool," the Decepticon says. Brakepad's eyes start to flash. Before he can take control of Bumblebee and Strongarm again, Rusty and Denny break into action.

"Now!" Rusty shouts. He yanks an oversized pair of novelty sunglasses out of his bag and places them snugly over Strongarm's optics. The lenses were sloppily painted black enough to block out Brakepad's hypnotic vision. Denny does the same to Bumblebee.

The Autobots stagger back. "What gives?" Bumblebee asks.

"Don't take them off!" Rusty replies. "They're...relaxation glasses! They're protecting you from Brakepad's powers, so he can't force you to exert yourselves!"

"Not cool, little dude," the Decepticon

responds. "How am I supposed to chill them out now?"

"Grim, kick that stasis pod over here!" Rusty yells. The Dinobot stirs slightly and returns to relaxing. "If you don't, Strongarm says she won't pull your trailer. You'll have to *walk all the way* back to the scrapyard." At the threat of too much labor, Grimlock stands up and gives the pod one massive kick. It drives

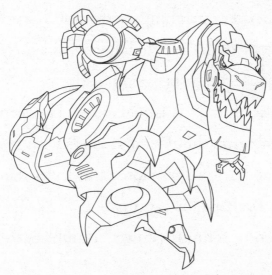

a rivet through the grass and comes to a stop in front of Brakepad's perch.

Denny taps the blinded Bumblebee on his arm to show him where to turn. "One last effort, Bee! Just knock this guy loose and you can power down until pigbots fly!" Rusty directs Strongarm toward the same goal. Gathering what little effort they have in them, Bumblebee and Strongarm pound Brakepad's perching spot and shake the Decepticon loose. He lands with a *THUNK!* in the working stasis pod below.

"Got him!" Rusty shouts. He leaps off Strongarm's shoulder and lands with two feet on the button that closes and locks the stasis pod. Brakepad is captured!

Denny climbs down Bumblebee's arm

and high-fives Rusty. "Fantastic plan, son! Although I'm sad to see these vintage novelty glasses get ruined...."

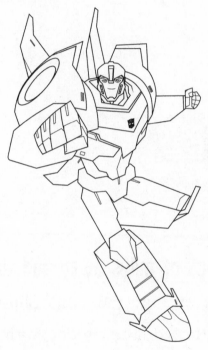

"Thanks, Dad," Rusty replies. "Now we just have to motivate these bots to drag the pod back to the scrapyard!"

Chapter 9

Thousands of miles away and thousands of feet up in the air, Slipstream—a samurai-trained alien robot with a secret mission on Earth—makes his way ahead of Loren Fortean's crew, rushing from hiding place to hiding place. Without knowing it, the humans have been walking straight up a booby-trapped path!

The diminutive Mini-Con has been defeating hidden dangers left and right to make sure the humans have an uneventful climb. Luckily for Slipstream, the sounds of his staff smashing turrets and slicing trip wires were covered by the raging winds.

"Start filming any dense flurries of snow," Loren Fortean commands. "We can run it later and say we saw a shape disappear into it, drum up some mystery." Fortean swallows hard and whispers to himself. "At this rate, the bigger mystery will be where I can find my next paycheck."

He and his crew are a mere hundred feet from Slipstream, but the visibility is so low that they can't tell! This suits Slipstream just fine. Less of a risk of his mission being uncovered.

Before long, Slipstream reaches a forking path. To the left, he can spot the now-familiar signs of buried traps. To the right, the snow looks clear. Quickly, before the humans can catch up, he uses his staff to smash the rocks on the left, collapsing the path so the humans can't easily follow him. With a quick leap over the rubble, Slipstream finds himself one step closer to finding Abominus, without the burden of babysitting Fortean!

On the other side of the summit, Optimus

and the Autobots near the conclusion of their

trek. They've defeated countless traps and have been making good time to compensate for their fall earlier, but losing Slipstream put them all in a dark mood. Not even Sideswipe can muster a joke.

As Everest's highest peak comes into view, Optimus's tread clinks against something hidden under the snow.

"Hold up, team," the Autobot leader commands. "I think I found something."

Optimus bends down and brushes away the snow to reveal a door embedded in the rock!

"This must be an entrance to Abominus's lair," Windblade says, examining the door. "Drift, Slick, our blades can probably wedge it open." The three bots drive their swords into the heavy metal and pull. With a serious effort, the door pops off its hinges, revealing a naturally occurring tunnel into the mountain. "That was probably the easy part. Expect Abominus to have plenty of other surprises waiting for us inside."

One by one, the bots file inside the tunnel. Jetstorm brings up the rear, casting one final glance around for any sign of Slipstream. The bots' optics take a moment to adjust to the lack of light. The tunnel curves and leads down.

"Is it strange that I'm nervous *because* we haven't run into any traps yet?" Sideswipe whispers.

"That's a smart instinct, Slick," Windblade responds. "Abominus isn't one to go light

on the weaponry. There should be more resistance down here."

As if on cue, Windblade's tread lands on a pressure-sensitive tile. Panels on the walls around them shift, revealing sharp spikes.

"Run!" Windblade shouts. The spikes begin shooting out of the wall in unpredictable patterns, ricocheting around the compact tunnel. Windblade, Drift, Jetstorm, and Sideswipe have no problem dodging the projectiles thanks to their acrobatic skills. Optimus, on the other hand, is too slow and bulky to evade them all.

Windblade rushes to the Autobot leader's side as the spike barrage finally subsides. "Optimus, are you injured?" Though Windblade already knows that Optimus wouldn't admit to an injury, especially if it might jeopardize the mission at hand.

"The spikes flew right past me," Optimus says. He winces as he stands up. "If that's the best Abominus can throw at us, he's going to be saying good-bye to his mountain sooner than he expected."

"Good thing that's not all I've got, eh?" a voice roars through speakers embedded in the rock. Suddenly, the floor below the bots retracts, plummeting them down another tunnel!

The bots land with a *CLUNK!* one after the other. Sideswipe is the first to stand up and take in his surroundings. The fall dropped the bots right in the middle of Abominus's lair—surrounded by heavy metal bars! Before Sideswipe can leap up, the roof of the cage slides into place.

"Trying to muscle in on my territory, are you?" Abominus says, stepping into view. The long-limbed Decepticon is shockingly white against the gray rock walls. A snowy environment is the perfect place for him to

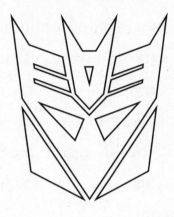

hide. "Can't be having that, oh no! A bot's home is his castle, and I aim to defend mine."

"You're a wanted fugitive, Abominus!" Windblade shouts at her captor. "I'm going to put you back in stasis."

Abominus whistles in response. "Oh ho ho, tough-bot behind bars, eh?"

Windblade reaches for her weapon, but before it leaves its holster, Abominus steps toward a nearby console. "Oh no, can't have that!" With one press of a button, the cruel Decepticon sends thousands of volts rushing through the cage.

The Autobots grimace and contort in discomfort. "Not this again!" Sideswipe says. "I've gotten enough charge today to last— oof!—a millennia."

"Plenty more where that came from!" Abominus threatens. "But if you bots behave yourselves, I'll let you have front-row seats to my grand finale."

Optimus throws himself against the massive bars of the cage. "What are you talking about, Decepticon?"

"The little life forms of this planet insist on climbing up *my* mountain and building their homes at the base of it," Abominus explains. "I've been placing explosives in key places all over the peaks. Once I'm done building the rest of these Energon bombs, I'm going to trigger them all at once and set off the avalanche to end all avalanches. *Boom!* No more intruders!"

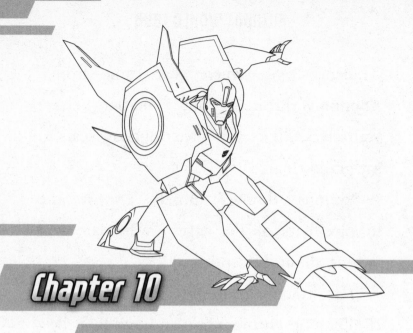

Chapter 10

"This is bad, team," Optimus says to his fellow bots.

"Yeah, no kidding, big guy," Sideswipe replies. "Abominus is probably going to strap us to those bombs when he blows up half the mountain!" Windblade and Optimus glare at the younger bot. "Plus, you know, all the humans who'd be caught in the avalanche…"

"Any luck working on the bars, Drift?" Windblade asks. After revealing his sinister plan, Abominus left to place more explosives around the summit. The Decepticon trusts his reinforced cage to keep the Autobots contained.

"Unfortunately, no," Drift replies. "Every time my blade glances the cage, it—ahh!—electrifies." The samurai Autobot recoils

from the shock and places his weapon back in its scabbard.

"And it's too risky to shoot my blaster in here," Optimus adds. "The electrified force field could send the blast ricocheting back."

"I'm running out of ideas," Windblade

says. "Abominus has a few loose screws, but he's dangerous. If he thinks blowing up half the mountain will help keep him isolated from outsiders, he'll do it. He wants to be left alone with only his weapons for company."

Sideswipe points at one of the video screens nearby. "Looks like Abominus might have another unexpected guest to deal with, then." Through the grainy video, the bots can just make out Slipstream wandering through the tunnel!

A few nanocycles later, Slipstream tumbles down the same hole in the floor that deposited the bots in their cage. With the roof now in place, the Mini-Con bounces off the top of the cage with only a momentary shock. He lands nearby, free from Abominus's trap.

"Brother!" Jetstorm and Slipstream shout simultaneously. Slipstream notices his master, too, and regains his composure. "Master Drift," Slipstream says with a bow. Drift nods his head slightly in return.

"I am glad you are safe," Drift says.

"Yeah, now get us out of here!" Sideswipe adds.

Optimus gets Slipstream up to speed on the situations while the Mini-Con searches the consoles nearby for a way to release the cage. After some tinkering, Slipstream finds the right button. The electrical hum of the bars dies down, and the roof recedes into the wall. One by one, the Autobots hoist themselves up and over.

"Good job, Slipstream." Freed from the cage, Optimus takes in his surroundings. Half-assembled booby traps lay all around the bots in various states of construction. "Okay, team, time to lay our own trap."

Sometime later, Abominus returns to his

lair. He glances at the bots in their cage and is satisfied to see them locked away as he left them. The orangutan-like Decepticon shakes great mountains of snow off his frame and sits in front of his wall of monitors.

"Soon enough I'll have the whole mountain to myself! No law-bots to bother me!" Abominus mumbles to himself. "The ultimate fortress! Eh, wait, what's this?" One of the Decepticon's camera feeds shows Slipstream entering the tunnel again!

"There's another one of you brain-rusted Autobots in my lair!" Abominus shouts. "Sit tight while I go deal with your friend." Abominus swings himself up into the tunnel using his massive arms. In his haste, he doesn't notice that the Autobots' cage no longer pulses with electricity.

The moment Abominus leaves, Slipstream darts out from under a pile of half-built turrets. "The looped video worked—he thinks I'm still in the tunnel!" he declares. Slipstream again retracts the roof of the cage. The bots climb out and dash to the nearby consoles.

As Windblade hacks into the explosives' controls and disables the Energon bombs placed around the mountain, the other bots watch Abominus barreling through the tunnels. While he was gone, they had time to reprogram his many booby traps to target only one bot: Abominus himself!

Through the video feed, the Autobots can see Abominus being blasted by his own turrets, swarmed by his own nanodrones, and tripped by his own hidden wires. If the feeds had audio, they'd surely hear a lot of choice Cybertronian words, too!

"Man, after the climb we had getting here, watching this Decepticon fall for his own traps makes me feel like a million credits!" Sideswipe exclaims.

"I deserve a million credits for this speedy hacking job," Windblade pipes in. "There, all the Energon bombs have been disabled. I programmed them all to slowly leak their explosive payload, too, so they won't trigger if someone stumbles on them someday."

"Good job, Windblade," Optimus says.

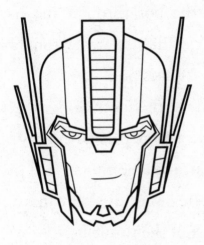

"Now it's time for the most satisfying trap of all." The Autobot leader presses a big red button on the command console. Within nanocycles, the bots hear a fast-approaching scream and a *THUD!* as Abominus lands in the cage. The roof slides shut, and the bars jump to life with electricity, trapping the Decepticon in his own cage.

"Don't worry, Abominus," Windblade says,

taunting the bot through the bars. "You're going to get the isolated stronghold of your dreams—a stasis pod!"

While the other bots work on getting Abominus into a more permanent cage, Sideswipe glances at the monitors. To his surprise, Loren Fortean and his crew have made it to the mouth of the tunnel!

"Hey guys, looks like we have a few more visitors," Sideswipe says. "Rusty's TV guy made it up here! But don't worry, I've got a plan...."

Back at the scrapyard, Rusty settles down in front of his television. It took a while to get

Bumblebee, Strongarm, and Grimlock back home with a captured Brakepad in tow, but by the time they arrived, the Decepticon's laziness-inducing effect had largely worn off.

Grimlock plops down next to Rusty in front of the TV. "I feel so recharged!" the Dinobot exclaims. "Maybe we can let that Decepticon out every once in a while for a spa day or something."

"I don't think so, 'bro-bot,'" Bumblebee says, joining his teammates. "I can't believe we acted so lazy. Strongarm is out back training overtime just to make up for it. At least the Decepticon is safely in stasis now. He can 'chill' until we find a way to return him and the other escaped prisoners to Cybertron."

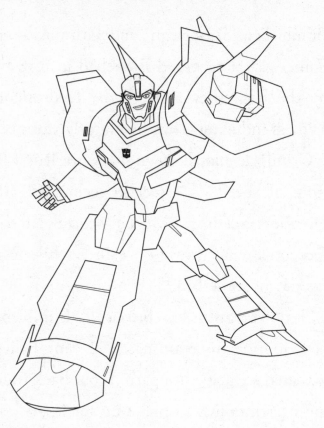

Rusty tries to quiet his Autobot pals. "That's great, you guys, but it's been an exhausting day, and I just want to watch *Beyond the*—"

"Great newt...noon...news!" Fixit proclaims, hurrying to join the bots and Rusty. "I just heard from Optimus and the others. They have successfully captured Abominus and are making their way down the mountain."

"What about Loren Fortean and his crew?" Rusty asks.

"Looks like you're about to find out," Fixit replies, pointing to the screen.

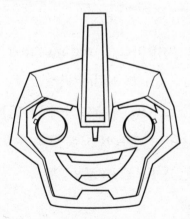

"That's right, faithful audience," the figure on the screen says. "My name is Loren Fortean, and I'm live-streaming from my climb down Mount Everest. Just moments ago, we brought you the very first verified audio recording of a real, live yeti! Play it back for everyone just tuning in, Ernie."

Rusty leans forward, eyes glued to the screen and ears alert.

"WOOOOOOO, LEAVE THIS PLACE!" the recorded voice booms.

"Wait a minute, I recognize that voice," Rusty says. "That's Sideswipe!"

"LEAVE MY MOUNTAIN AND NEVER RETURNNNNN!" the voice goes on. "HI, RUSTYYYYYYY!"

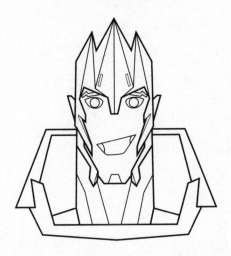

Rusty cracks a huge smile. The screen cuts back to Loren Fortean.

"That's right, dear viewers. I, Loren Fortean, am the first person to capture yeti audio on tape. I'm not sure who this 'Rusty' is, but you can bet I'll be investigating it now that I've been renewed for three more seasons!"

The Trials of
Optimus Prime

Turn the page
for a sneak peek!

Chapter 1

A massive red-and-blue semitruck barrels through a narrow canyon, sounding its booming horn like a rallying cry.

Three other vehicles race close behind: a boxy blue police cruiser, a sleek red sports car, and a compact yellow coupe with black stripes.

At the opposite end of the canyon, an army of imposing figures stands armed and ready to fight. The semitruck and its convoy spit clouds of dust into the air as spinning wheels tear across the sandy ground.

Moments before the truck collides with the edge of the army, its wheels leave the ground, its shape twists and changes in the air, and it reveals itself to be much more than just a vehicle—it's actually a robot in disguise!

"Autobots, attack!" the robot shouts, landing so one massive foot crushes an enemy to the ground.

The three other vehicles follow suit, lifting into the air and changing into robot modes of their own!

The army of foes reveals itself to be

composed of snarling, angular robots of a much more sinister variety: Decepticons. These terrible foes brandish wicked blades and maces.

The four Autobots stand together as a team, pushing back attackers and knocking them off one by one with energy blasters and swords. The red-and-blue leader calls the shots and looks out for his teammates.

"Bumblebee, on your left!" the leader warns, directing the yellow-and-black bot to block an incoming blow.

CRASH!

The parried Decepticon staggers back and takes out a few of its brethren as it falls.

"Sideswipe, take out that cannon!"

The nimble red bot catapults over a pile

of rocks and slices through a pair of foes readying a massive energy cannon.

THUD!

The cannon hits the canyon floor and blasts back a whole fleet of Decepticons.

CHOOM!

"Strongarm, create a perimeter for us!"

VROOM!

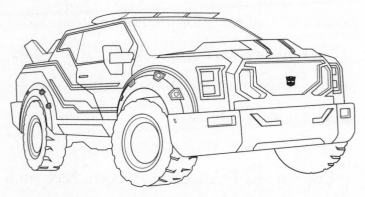

The broad-shouldered blue bot changes back into her vehicle mode and plows through the Decepticons, clearing a space for the Autobots to make a unified stand.

The enemies continue to swarm, but the four Autobots work together like one well-oiled machine.

"Good job, Autobots! But this Decepticon horde doesn't seem to be getting any smaller. We need backup."

With a flick of his wrist, the Autobot leader summons an energy shield to hold off the aggressive attackers. He speaks into the communicator embedded in his other arm.

"Fixit, we could use some extra feet on the ground right about now!"

The communicator crackles and hisses.

As if on cue, a shape darkens the sky above

the Decepticon infantry. Its shadow grows as it plummets toward the ground.

BOOOOOM!

The formidable figure smashes into the gathered Decepticons, flattening the unlucky enemies caught beneath it. The impact emits a shockwave that knocks many more off their feet.

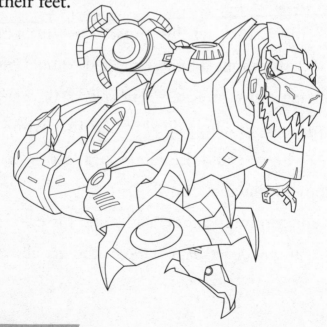

"Thanks for dropping in, Grimlock," the leader quips.

A huge black-and-green Dinobot climbs out of the crater he just formed, grins, and joins the rumble.

"Any time!" he replies, stampeding through the horde.

The leader can't help it: He cracks a smile, too.

Even as the enemy army doubles then triples in size, he is confident that his team can stand strong against the forces of evil! He continues to bark orders and provide covering fire while countless Decepticons pour into the canyon.

Then, out of nowhere, a large swell of new enemies separates the huddled

Autobots. The leader can no longer watch his teammates' backs. He hears a pained cry ring out and then get cut short.

"Sideswipe!"

The red bot has fallen and is quickly covered by Decepticons.

Then another scream echoes through the canyon.

"Strongarm, no!" Optimus cries.

The blue police-bot drops against the canyon wall and is similarly overtaken.

The leader's resolve begins to crack, and the confidence he felt mere moments ago leaves him. He searches through the crowd for his remaining teammates. It's not too late to rally and force the Decepticons back....

A deep groan and an earthshaking thud tell him that the large Dinobot has been defeated, too.

Beating back Decepticons on every side, the leader pushes through to the yellow-and-black bot's position. Blades slice and maces smash against his plating as he prioritizes the search for his last standing teammate over his own safety.

Cannons fire around him into the canyon walls, throwing dust and rock shards into the air. Optimus hears a familiar cry and sees a blur of yellow fall toward the ground.

"Bumblebee!" the leader shouts. With a wide swoop of his sword, he knocks back a swarm of enemies to reveal the crumpled shape of the last remaining member of his team.

"No, not you, too," he whispers, kneeling beside his friend. The yellow-and-black bot barely moves.

"Optimus..."Bumblebeestrugglestospeak.

The leader looks down at his injured comrade.

"Optimus, the others..."

The dazed Decepticons pick themselves up and surround the duo. Escape is impossible.

The Autobot leader, Optimus, is soon covered on all sides, stumbling under the combined weight of his faceless assailants.

He struggles and strains to hear what Bumblebee has to tell him over the din of the Decepticon army.

And suddenly, the message is clear:

"Optimus . . . you failed us!"

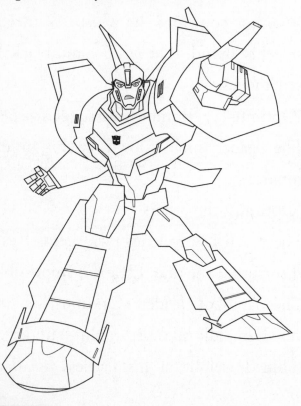